BLOCK LEGEND PAPER
BY THE TON VI

KEVIN GREEN

authorHOUSE®

AuthorHouse™
1663 Liberty Drive
Bloomington, IN 47403
www.authorhouse.com
Phone: 833-262-8899

Published by AuthorHouse 11/16/2020

ISBN: 978-1-6655-0815-5 (sc)
ISBN: 978-1-6655-0814-8 (e)

Print information available on the last page.

This book is printed on acid-free paper.

WHEN IT ALL ENDS

I wonder what will we do when it all ends, running through life with the sky falling; look out below catch me in the wind no time to cry wolf, nowhere to run, nowhere to hide, we all are dying on the inside with no time to hide, grab the nine and AK with no place to ride, what does it matter if we're all dying on the inside, emotions run deep, we swallow our pride to hide the feelings that lie inside, hoping it doesn't all end, when it all ends trying to stay afloat when the sky starts falling, what do you do when the worlds collide, everyone fighting for life, step on, or be stepped on. I wonder if any of it will ever matter after we're all gone. Life goes on and moves on to the next chapter, we might lay in peace the next morning after, trying to keep it all together during this natural disaster. Knowing what happens now determines what happens after watching the tears fall, watching the world turns against us all. Watching everyone for safety as the sky falls came, who knew the worlds would turn against us all. Running over you all, at the end of the world it's save me <u>fuck yall.</u> They are trying to step on me to stand tall, running in circles holding unto life, trying to stay strong, even at the end of life, life goes on; hoping life doesn't give up on me when it's time for the world to move on came life goes on. Watching planes fall and crash and burn to ashes, ash to ash and dust to dust killing the next man for the life we lost, listening to the chaos that the world brings, listening to the flames sing. I wonder what will we do when it all ends, trying to stay afloat with the sky falling. Life is life, until life is death. It's hard to breathe when you are running out of breath. I am not sure if it was a metro or something from once before, all we can do is hold on tight and endure. Life will never be like once before, If they have change the value of money, we'd all be poor, trying to live life like once before, trying to stay out of the rain when it starts to pour, run what for I can't breathe and these ashes fill my lungs, waters turn acidic and blood runs cold, traumatized by life as the world unfolds. Life's cold and it's getting colder, running from mother nature. I think God told her, their looking for payback, they gave life just to take life back, a little test of your own medicine, take that we're not the only ones that can't grow back, blood and tears mix in with this world of sin. I hope we're prepared to win, when it's time to end, the world stops the spin, something from once before to bring this life to an end, as small as we are we can't win the price of life for living in sin. I wonder what will we do when our world comes to an end, I wonder if we can ever start over again. Life is life until Life moves on again, I wonder how it will all end, watching the worlds collide as the sky starts falling, fed up, God and Mother Nature put us all in. Life is life, without life who cares who's falling Payback I'm all in. The sky is falling, the sky is falling, that death's calling. I'm all in where will you be when the world comes to an end. I hope when it's all over, I can breathe again.

POEM: MR. DEALER

POKER FACE

Playing the cards never knowing which cards will be played next hoping for the card that will give me the upper hand, a winning chance to make them all amty up, not being able to see the next card I pick up, hoping the aces are on my side, hoping for a royal flush watching the cards slide. No jokers in the deck we play wish aces high watching the hands of the dealer every time my cards slide bye. Playing the hand I'm dealt throwing in my chips, hoping for the chance to stack sky high everytime the cards flip. Slide me. Another Mr. Dealer and count me in playing throat cut and I play to win. No grins, now frowns. Keeping my poker face on at all times, not time for second guessing when its chips on the line. So pass me another Mr. Dealer and let the cards fly bye, poker face on no emotion stacking sky high sticking to the rules and regulations everytime the cards slide bye, making them untie up, playing cards right, knocking down the competition. No Mr. Dealer I'm not done yet stacking up my chips everytime I bet waiting for any signs, watching for the coming of dripping sweat. Keeping my game face on everytime I play, waiting for Mr. Dealer to reshuffle the deck. So slide me another Mr. Dealer, the best hand I await, starving for the game, waiting for my next hand and I can hardly wait, loving everytime the cards flip, so slide me another one and Mr. Dealer don't slip, hoping for the Royal Flush everytime, eyes on the cards and stacking chips on my mind, no second guessing I have to play my cards right, holding the best hand with no competition in sight, untie up. I just might keep my game face on, playing the right with my poker face on. So slide me another one Mr. Dealer and give me a hand that can understand playing the game right, holding my cards in my hand.

It's cold in these streets but somebody got to eat out on the grind all the time, trying to make ends meet living in a place where its hard to compete, out here pinching pennies living the life I chose, staying on the grind with an eye on foes. I gotta eat so the eat so the hard life is the wife I chose out here on these mean streets, its me before ho's, just me being me, living the life I chose, out here in these mean streets with an eye on foe's.

POEM

Counting the tears falling down my cheek

Watching my life fall apart right in front of me,

Trying to put my life back together

But the pieces don't fit.

My life is falling apart and my knees feel weak

Trying to put it together but I can't find the beat

My heart skips a beat, waiting the tears fall down my cheek

Putting my life back together but it feels like missing a piece,

Its feel like my heart and soul are on fire,

Somebody, help me sooth my soul,

Watching my world fall apart knowing I'm not in control

Hoping I can put my life on hold,

Hoping for somebody to hold me, console me,

Help me in my time of need

And never let go of me

Someone to love me,

To need me,

Someone to know me,

Believe me, love me, forgive me,

And wont deceive me, watching the tears fall down my cheek

Hoping for someone to catch me when my body feels weak,

When I'm weak in the knees,

Hoping for someone to console me and fulfill my needs.

Feeling so lonely, I don't know what to do,

So I wrap up my tears and send them to you

Feeling so helpless I don't know what to do,

Feeling so sick for loving you,

Watching my tears fall on,

My pillow wishes they were you,

Staring at the wall seeing visions of you,

So sick feeling over you,

I don't know what to do

Sick In love,

Falling over you,

And I don't know what to do

Yo, let's right

Yo, let's right

Step by step, right

Yo, let's right

Yo, let's right

Take one step right

Yo, let's right

Dance ship right

Yo, let's right

Yo, let's right

TRAPPED IN A BOX

Around to hear my constant yells,

Nobody to help me in my search for life,

Nobody here to help me find the light,

Nobody here to help me in my search for sight,

Trapped in this box, trying to claw the light

Suck fear, not knowing if my actions were for nothing

I can feel the end creeping in

I can feel the messenger of death closing in

Like the wind blowing over my skin

I cant give up

This cant be the end for me

Trapped in this box, trying to hold me for eternity

With unwelcome company stuck in this box

With only my bones to accompany me

I can feel something in on the other side,

Hands soaked with life, I can feel the lights

Hoping for a shallow grave,

Not ready for the afterlife

I can feel the end closing in

Trapped in this box, living in the world I'm in

Running out of time, taking deep breathes,

Crawling my way out, trying to cheers death

I found my way out, skin to bone,

Clawing to find my way out

I finally found the lights

Trapped in this box

From dark to light

Finally free as bye living in the afterlife

I pledge alegance to my balls

For busting the bucks bitches

While my dick stand tall

Busting nuts after all while I stand

Thank God, I still remain a Man

With my hand over my heart,

With one hand on the back,

While I stand busting all over bucks

When I can think of God for making me a man

Busting off the back of bitches when I can

I can feel the end closing in

With no light in sight

Hoping life in the afterlife

Stuck in the dark waiting for glimmer of light

There is no room out here for me,

No space to breathe, no room to grow,

No way out, no truth to the life,

I live only lies and deception

Falsehood and fiction

No truth in the life,

I live except for the life I live

Trapped by lies that cross the lines of life,

Hoping for life in the afterlife

With no end in sight

Hoping for the end to close in

And take away all the lies that surrounds me

A life of lies that can creep up to drown me

While I can feel the end closing

In with no end in sight

Hoping for end of torments and strains of life

Hoping for a life with a reason to live

With more meaning

Then this hoping for much more

More life than this

Surrounded by lies with no end

Hoping for something better waiting at my end

I can feel the end closing in

Waiting for something better than life I'm in.

Trapped in a box with no way out

I can feel the end closing in

Trapped with no way out

Stuck in the box I'm in

I can feel the end getting close

Sucking the life away

Stuck in this box of fright

Watching the time drift away

Slipping away, with hardly any room

To move or maneuver

Wondering how I did end up here

My brains more stupid

Living in ignorance, fear and fright

Stuck in a box with no light

Not knowing if outside of this box is day and night

Stuck, frightened,

Short light, driving me to insanity

I can feel the end closing in

With the cold breeze flowing over my skin.

I can't win trapped in a box with no way out

Trapped in a box with no way out

Living in fear I can feel the end near,

Sucking the life from every breath I take

trying to claw myself with every move I make,

digging in feeling my skin rip,

while I try to rip through.

I feel the end closing in as the wood splitters my bodily tissue

Trying to claw myself out

Feeling my blood soak through, dripping on face

Stuck, trapped in this box

Running out of space

With the taste of my own seeping in

Hating my life and the box I am in

Running out of time, running out of space

Stuck in this box

Feeling the tears running down my face

I can't breathe. I can't see.

All I can do is hear the dreadful sound of scrapping wood to bone

And the sound of the beat of my heart and the cries of agony

Fright and fear, echoes bouncing off the mood

Landing down my ear,

Such fear, such fright

Trapped in this box,

Pleading for my own life

Stuck in the box with no way out

Trapped with no lights

I cant wish feeling the blood from the top of the box

Dripping on my chin,

Feeling the wind from my own lungs

Coating my chest

I can feel the end getting nearer,

I'm running out of breath,

What did I do wrong

To have my world end like this

Trapped in a small box with no room to move

Laying on my own

Clawing through the top of the box,

Crying, searching for home

Trapped in this box with no lights'

In a world on its own

Trying to call out of this box which is not my home

There must be a way out of this death trap

Clawing at the top of the trying to find my way out

Skin ripped to the bone

Skinned alive, trying my best to claw myself out

Trying my best to survive

I can feel the end closing in

Offering the end of me

Trapped in this box with no light, I can't see

I can only feel the thumping of my own heart

Thump! Thump! Thump! Thump!

And the tears falling down my face,

And the blood soaked

Pine shavings, falling all over my face, my hands numb

Then bones clawing hot skin

I can feel the end closing in

Hoping to make it out of the box of hell in nobody

BEAUTIFUL

And you can have this life of mine, tared and torn by life

And you can have this heart of mine, cold and lifeless compared to you,

I value none, a life full of heartache and heartbreak.

Shadowed by death, and weighed down by the stress of the world,

longing for someone as beautiful as you,

May I fall in love with you,

I would leave it all for you,

Would I be insulting if I said,

I love you,

A star to shine bright,

Like a moth to a flame I'm attracted to light,

Like the moon and sun that brings light to life,

A beauty beyond sight,

A miracle of life beyond my reflection in the mirror,

My clarity in the mist of sadness,

Could this be the end of the madness?

The beginning of the end of one's heart so cold,

Wiping away tears older than time,

I would gladly trade my life, for this beauty of mine,

My own star to shine

With her on my arm,

This world feels limitless, a warming of a heart so heartless,

Take hold this life of mine, torn by time,

restless in the space until this beauty's mine.

Hold on tight,

I'll never let go,

She's priceless in every way as real as flesh can be,

I imagine an image of her along side of me.

I wonder if I can bring this fantasy to life,

She feels as real as me, longing for what could be,

But how does one catch a shooting star,

Flying faster then light, powerful enough to turn day to night,

A gift of life, to bring my heart to life,

I offer you my heart, and the key to me,

And my worthless life.

Separate from the pain that stains the soul,

She's perfection, as perfect as time,

Now willing to give up this lifetime of mine.

I'm the most valuable player in two states, loving how my tea jumps from state to state, bi-coastel to season my steak, sincerely that nigga you love to hate.

Entirely the world's most hated, even the voices in my head hate me, it wil take more than your sinal tape to break me. I'm the most hated nigga alive, with spinel came to shoot. Strapped up from head to toe, now tell me how much you hate me, even my nine's suck'a free, like I'd let this niggas sucka me, like I wouldn't let your bitch suck for me, and tell your bitch one nut, aint enough nut for me. She can suck for free, now they know why they hate on me, I'm sugar free, bitch made nigga, <u>aint no bark for mine, except for mine, I'm a boss baby, just keep that in mind</u>. I got business in every state, like a Dope friends, I friend for cake. Balling on the block with more cream to take, with more bread than the average niggas who just scream and take like frosting. I friend for cake a sinner by nature. Cause I too friend to take, <u>have you ever seen a nigga, with his hand on the trigga, ready to blast.</u> I am something more than your average ass nigga finding for cash. I need more. Cause I said so, cause I've been there and done that, I'm a boss baby, simply because I toat that, flying over head with lead, with Feds listening to everything said to me, fuck them niggas, them niggas dead to me. All I need is myself and a quarter key, hoping the Feds don't take this life from me. Cause I am like I suppose to be, turning life to death like BIC = money with an ego, like a blunt to ash, True to the Game and all about my cash, that's why you shoot first and then mash the gas, Your Dope Dealing MVP, all you have to do is untie up to find me, cause time is cash, this one goes out to all my Dope Friends who fiend for gas, Bi Coastel, jumping from state to state,

Sincerely, your that nigga you love to hate (World's Most Hated Nigga) I'm the realest nigga alive and you not it's a sin to let these bitches niggas profit off dope spot. The realest nigga alive.

ALONE

Alone again, gone and forgotten, the end seems close to me, empty, and hallow draped in the skin. I'm in a shell of what once was, a fraction of self, my life seems to be just a memory, how could the light of life remember me, just a memory to be, left with nothing where did the substance of life go, carried away by the winds, as the wind blows, to and fro, where did my life go. So empty and hallow, waiting for the winds to blow life my way, so empty inside. Today, hoping the stress and strife of life fly away, tempted by death with black clouds over head, remembering exactly with heart to what the winds said, happiness is in the heart of the ones who keep love close to heart if this is the end, where do I start, loving, love as art, Alone again searching for a feeling of heart

Gone and Forgotten

From Me

To you

Here's a piece of My Heart

POEM

Pleasure and Pain, as the rain comes my way, hoping we live to die another day, will when the madness end, trapped by memories of the past, praying for hope, and good fortune, searching for the Key to happiness to erase the madness that lies within, buried between the skin I'm in, waiting for good time to surface once again. Tempted by sin, as my words of wisdom are blown away. By the wind, hoping never to sin again, I'm only flesh, and bone as my torment, and madness roams free, listening deeply to what these wise words showed me. There is no whining between the lines of life and death, life controlled by faith, time and space lived by the worlds affirmation to life, enduring life's pleasures, and pain until the end of life, as the rain come, show me the way to heaven's gate, and watch me disappear into paradise after life, tell me why must one suffer to enjoy the True pleasures of Life. Waiting for happiness to come way, knowing this pain and torment will end before life's end watching the rainfall again, praying for happiness before the end as my life is wasted away by the wind until I begin again.

He's a cop! He's a cop, and she's a cop too! I do not trust nobody that's why I had the white boy slide through.

I am hated by the President and the Feds on my tail, because I'm addicted to Dope Money, and high clientele, now I got real estate T-shirts, and CDs for sell, turn talking all the way to the bank, watching my money talk, knowing one day, I'll be outlined in white chalk, living the life of a straight hood nigga, is the only life for me, if you want the best deal in town, you can buy for me, sowing I up like seamstress is the life to me.

He's a cop, He's a cop, and she's a cop too, can't trust nobody when that white bitch slides through, He's a cop, He's a cop, and she's a copt too 2 for 30 you heard me, so hurry up and Cop 2.

Gone is sixty seconds as I blast off my desert eayal stuck to me even when I take my cash off, duet taped and wrapped for life, and I'm off again, soaring past the S.O. then from a balled like me. You can get anything you ask for, consuming life to live life, taking heads for a price, and I'm off again, with my gun smoking in the winds, and I'm gone again, until it's time to blast off again, with my strap, strapped to the spine of me, just letting you into the mind of me, you could never be the nigga. I'm trying to be forever real and sucka free don't test me, putting holes in bitch niggas for free, I'm your Dope Dealer Killa, and the Games MVP aint another nigga alive like me, I shoot first so catch fire, your life is for the taking if you aint down to ride, busting my 45 from side to side put your glocks in the air and show them how the G's ride, like 3 6 Mafia twisting my blunts from side to side, rain, sleet, and hell's show there's always money on the block. Along with these scheming ass nigga that scheme to plot, all over profit and respect, and a million dollar dope spot, break a billion dollars down like I was breaking down a block, a million sold not told like I was breaking down, a glock, getting head from a chicken hear in my Johnny on the spot, then spit away, clean in my candy apple drop, a million sold not like emotion lotion and my favorite lemon drop, all from slanging cream, gripping my sour apple glock, blowing up the spot, cause my cherry beating up the block, gone in sixty seconds blasting off from my dope spot. Watching my cherry bottom drop, me and my candy coated cock, a billion sold not told off your local neighborhood Dope Spot.

Beyond the looking glass, an image that brightens the soul, a love yet to hold, a connection as old as time. Will you be mine? Beyond the looking glass, lies a love older than time, older than rhythm and rhyme, her beauty never changes unlike the sands of time, could she be mine, this beauty that lies beyond the looking glass, thinking of loves face as the years past, knowing love the last eternally, generations past, while my beauty remains the same, love more beautiful, then the sweetest wine, more nourishing the lifes rain, with beauty strong enough to numb the strongest pain, this beauty of mine, valued more than this life of mine, my reflection of life beyond the looking glass, loving her beauty remains as our years pass.

You told me your heart was meant for me,

I thought we were meant to be,

I thought my heart was meant for you,

soulmates to be,

you said I was the light of your life,

meant for life to share,

promising a heart meant not to share,

like the moon colliding with the sun to become one,

what would life be like without the moon and sun,

You told me I could love you for life,

Instead you but a pricetag on a much priceless life.

I thought you were mine until the end of time,

When I wish to share with you this life of mine,

Do you wish me gone and forgotten before sunshine,

I thought your heart was as warm as mine, Mrs. Bitter Sweet

Life without Love like yours will leave me brittle and weak.

Love's gone but never forgotten,

I thought I was meant for you, and you were meant for me,

Because we were meant to be,

But you told me your heart was never meant for me,

So cold and heartless,

How could this be,

I guess I was meant for you,

But you were never meant for me.

Fuck a bitch that don't follow suit,

Kicking bitches out the cape with two to boot,

Can't fuck a bitch for free no more,

Nigga, I'm in it for the lost,

Bitches make dollars and dollars make cents,

And who said pimping was dead,

A bitch cant squeeze a dollar,

If she's a hoe then let it be,

With my pimp hand on the side of me,

Like you aint Know,

As soon as your bitch leave,

My bitch is creeping in the window,

Like bitch to dough off a pinch of snow,

Collecting dough like Don wond and Fill move,

Still pimping in my steel toe come and holla at a pip,

Slap five t make five,

All of a limp,

You simp,

Like Mac Dre pushing ho for dough as I cognac sip,

Life is great to me passing hos through the VIP

Yes my nigga you should holla at me,

I'm all about cop.

I just cant help myself, I guess it's just the Boos in me,

Cause I P.I.M.P. for a good time you should Holla at me

Cause hating on these nigga's that fuck for free

Cause I P.I.M.P., P.I.M.P., P.I.M.P.,

These bitches on deck, yes Holla at me

And fuck all the police, because the police wasn't never meant to protect me

Because I'm saucy ass fuck and as Black as can be,

That's why they stay hating on me,

Riding on my Chevrolet eating a 10 piece bucket of Spicy KFC,

Forever sucka free,

Like this life was meant for me, I don't know what else to say I guess it's just the pump in me,

I don't know what else to say I guess it's just the pimp in me,

Told the 50 there aint no pimping me,

Your just a busta that don't fuck for free as I slang chicken from the VIP

I'm true to life aint no fucking with me,

I guess it's just the Boss in me,

Getting a bitches ho dollars for me,

I'm a boss pimping you should holla at me,

Like a bill collector I wasn't every dollar you see,

And it's always cash first like C.O.D. telling bitches not to fuck niggas who fuck for free,

Pushing ho like snow for dough,

With bitches that snow blow, to money it aint nothing for a bitch to blow,

Controlling your lifestyle and everywhere you attempt to go and I'll pimp your ho,

As I cadilac drift and cognac sip you Ho,

Letting niggas know

This is how your cadilac pimp your Ho, now let's go!

Paranoia, Psycotic with Bi-Polar tendencies, riding fully loaded so I know you're feeling these, gambling my life with Killas and Dope Dealers with major falonnies, aint no testing these, dusting off these bitches like flees, nigga please, aint a nigga alive with nuts like these. Turning snow flakes to G's, flipping OZ for cheese with OG's grinding with nuts like these, dodging these falonnies, Fuck with me, your million dollar hitter, like a Californian card Member, I'm bomb and then some, you lose some you win some, break a bitch down for her check and then cum. I pimped the Dope Game and then Won, a million out a mole hill and the Ton laughing with these niggas now, like Big Pun, filling these bitches for fun, money over heard so real niggas but lead, cause hollows only be red, it's best to keep a Billion Dollar Plan in the head like a million dollar bitch in the bed, you hear real niggas talk but aint heard nothing we said, real to heart like I bleed Red, Would these niggas do bleed like us, because of the gunz we cock back I'd bust, breaking down cake and cutting down dust, and God knows I'm the only nigga I trust, because most of these niggas are scandalous, up the Game now the Police can't handle the robber backing chicken scratch stack and stack, 300 100 dollar bills like paper back, I'm a boss aint not changing that, like infared when I'm aiming that, that's your bitch and I'm claiming that you might be the nigga I'm aiming at, a Hood nigga for life and I'm claiming that I'm a wild boss aint now changing that, put a glock to a nigga head now, Billion sold not told, Boss aint no changing that, Welcome to the Dope Man Show.

Witness the snow, witness the dough, witness the lime light the shine, the gilts, the grind, keep this money on my mind, witness the drugs, the crime, this world is mine, all about a nick he to a dime, witness the nuts so grind, always keep a buck to mine, with these nuts of mine, witness bitches swallowing without a motherfucking dime, just talk to a bitch and you'll be fucking in no time, like a white boy with a shine, I don't give a fuck about nobody I'm all about this million dollar grind, witness a nigga, rise to the top with a stop watch, I'm top notch, like a top notch, witness these dollars roll in non stops, there are more to rap and hip hop then nap and Hip Hop, there's more to life, more numbers than the dot on dice, I'm a boss baby written these hits to life, more to life, and this gift to Life, witness a nigga with his life on the line, I could hustle and a dollar on a dime, these haters could never stop my shine, pimping bitch off a mutherfucking dime, talking with this bitch under the Californian sunshine. Witness a nigga dodging the one time, like a crack hand off a dime, I'm a baker baby, money only takes time, busy running from the one time, witness the lime, crawling down the motherfucking pipeline, witness a nigga making a million off a rhyme, all you need is a pinch of snow to shine like breaking down a billion dollar worth of dope down to all dimes, nigga this world is mine.

TALKING DOPE SHIT WITH MY CLIP AND MINE

Watching these bitches niggas show them my asses, knowing I hate the smell of bullshit listening to these haters talk shit but really don't shit. I'd rather listen to sounds of on play and let my nine spit, I don't give a fuck about what you said, I'm the shit, put my dick in her throat because she forgot who she fucks with, bomb like sour diesel and blueberry cheese, like pac out there dodging these felonies. Engulfed by cheese and purple trees, just to keep my mind at ease grew up around hustlas, Dope dealers, killas, thieves, I'd Gees, pimp slapping any nigga to hate on these. Boss on your Block with glock hoping they hate on these, fuck to Bad Black Filipino, and Japanese, now I understand why these haters hate on these. You talk about rap I'd rather not, since these niggas licked me imaging your spot, whether you're ready or not, everything in your pocket with my pistol glock, kicking on doors with my pistol cocked, ain't left of these niggas when my pistol stop, pissing on these bitches since I hit the top making these dance when I pistol pop, praying to your GOD to get this shit to stop running, through these niggas pockets with a pistol pop, I got this ink on my head and I cant get this shit to stop, serving dope friend without a pit to stop, fucking your pitch I wont even pretend to stop, right on my lap is where I keep my pistol cocked seen the police on your street, that's why I missed the drop. I'm so gone I can't get this shit to stop. Keeping my nine to spine in mind, hoping to put a glock to mind. I bet these niggas Dope Spit don't spit like dine, talking dope shit, with my clip, and nine, strapped up to my hip and my spine, blowing bitches away like I lost my mine, these niggas came in. So I am coming to take mine, me and my clip and my pistol shine, loving the hustle, the grip, my clip and the grit the grind, fully loaded like a clip to mind just another nigga cursed with the gift of crime, written these million dollar hits with this twist of lime, a wise man told me you need a pinch to shine, I'm the realest nigga walking so put this hit to mind, I'm just talking dope shit with my clip and my nine, Kicking down doors with this piece of mine.

Put a price on life, most of these niggas ain't worth shit, out there slanging cream spitting this Dope shit know most of these niggas once shit, Jon the block collecting these dollars and cents, welcome to the Dope man show, I push cream and I push snow, I push lean, and I push low, put a pound of kush away all on the low Balling, expecting these niggas to switch you already know with a little cump, change to show, hustling went from weed to blow like I changed the show, like I changed the show, counting down dirty money so I changed dough, heroin to snow like I changed the blow, fuck you, you owe and I still toat steel and stand my toe to toe, addicted to Dope money like a Dope friend to snow, I'm a Baller Baby so let them know, and I'm fucking your bitch on the low, so now I'm in and out your ho, licking a niggas in and out with dough, dollars make cents, and all that back stabbing shit is email event my nine's heaven sent, niggas in deep water and I ain't bailing shit, most of these niggas be telling shit, while I'm on your block pushing dope selling shit, 5 to 10 and 10 to 100, mix and mash the shit and running it, safety off the cockbaked with mash to gun it is been there and done that cause I done it, remember me I'm the real nigga you pretend to be, most of these niggas doing shit to me, this page is something like a million dollar spit to me, I'm the nigga you pretend to be, fucking bitches in abandoned buildings, never doing business with woman and children, cause I push white bitch and children listening to my dirt block life living cutting down birds on Thanksgiving, thank God I'm still living, life ain't nothing like it used to be, if you get caught up I hope you don't mention me, still the Boss plays you pretend to be, Hoping my life don't put an end Home these niggas ain't got no love for me, so I cock back and blast for this 5 to 10 for me like Tennessee I'm something like ten a Key, the realest nigga alive like you're suppose to be, if them niggas to get to tall for you send them to me I'm a true Boss you see, props for any nigga to put and end to me, these nigga said these nigga's living the life to me, is all until I fall fuck ya'll, my mine milla meter stand stall it's me and my chop verse ya'll, shooting until I fall fuck ya'll, I'm all in like a nigga doing life in the penn, loving this life I'm in, it it's about bread count me in, I'm all about the win, rolling up loud putting bomb in the wind, fucking with killas that don't pretend, pushing weight to this is the life I'm in, like 7 I win, cutting heads off at the chin, a Boss, to Boss life loving this life I'm in, tell homie I'm all in if I get send a playing pack to the penn, loving this life I'm in, as long as that money comes through I win, fuck with me, even when tem boys come through strapped up to get me, even when them boys come through strapped up to get me, you with me, I'm all in. I'm ready to Die life pac, biggie and left eye, I'm prepared to Die, my life's almost too much too handle all I need is me and my extra clip and my chrome grip to handle because most of these niggas ain't shit to me.

I think my mind skipped a beat, blowing bomb from cheek to cheek, pistol on lap not under seat as my mind skips on a beat, machine making nine again repeat bullets bounce from street to street, flat line a bitch without a beat, can't remember nothing like my brain lost a beat. I'm not like when you mix the Dope with the street, my pistol on lap cause I will not use it when it's under the seat, I'll change the world and I'll change your life, I'll change the Dope, and I'll change the price, just sit back and notice how Dope changed your life paid dues on the block watching lay turn to night, like watching this bomb seed turn into night, I'm watching bitch duck and hide as my nine spits the light, I don't give a fuck about the hater and your gifts to life, and you can tell OG, I wonder if you remember me, attracted to Dope Money and your style of life, if I get put down you would send for me, just to bring a playback to life, ain't nothing stronger than love if you raise it right, I keep my game wrapped tight, baby I was meant for you, I'm a Boss Baby you know how I do, her pussy so good my heart skipped a beat, still blowing bomb from cheek to cheek, swelling up her pussy even after her knees get weak, keep this between me and you, like OGs do, this nuts for you, as my heart skips a beat, I pack bitches, that pack heat, putting money in the street, like Dope to the beat, without cash you can't eat, still pimping the game like slim from fill more street, Holla at me.

Ball till I Fall, ain't nobody game me shit, out there on the grind just to pay the rent, my life is as hard as it gets, ain't no love for a nigga like me, ain't another nigga like me, these hater plot and plan to take me out, once you're in there ain't no out. Cause niggas friend for Dope Money and Clout, and the next mark to out, forever the realest nigga walking, I guess it's the Boss in me. They don't understand how much these brick costing me, a lost ain't just a lost to me, Balling in the eyes of thy enemy, strapped tight, my whole life's busta free, I guess the money got best of me wondering why these haters keep testing me, this is my life through the scope, just because I push Dope, living with crosshiers tattooed on my back, I'm worth more than get back, give me the cash, the devil can keep the rest of me, sick of these devils testing me, making sure these pigs don't get the best of me, now what's left of me, high on life, grinding and paying the price, forever sucka free these haters was never meant for me. I'm a Boss, chopping down every pack they sent to me, a live wire for hire. I'm just another nigga avoiding the fire, busting head so ante up, firing up bomb, drinking till I throw up, busting on niggas when they run up, adding another stack to the flame every time I come up, adding another stack to the flare every time I come up, I wonder if this life was meant for me, this could be it for me, another million dollar hit for me, just check out all the hittas they sent for me, listening to full clip meant for me, this could be it for me wondering what happen to help GOD sent for me, hope my real niggas stay lit for me, pour out some liquor when I'm gone, I grip stacks, and I grip chrome when it's on might not see a nigga later on, this might be my maker calling me Home, popped, one to the dome, I'm so in love with my chrome, Balling, blazed up in the zone, because nigga when it's on it's on, a Boss whenever I roam. These white boys would rather see me slang Dope, rather me being Heroin and Coke, then shove my dick down a white bitch throat, once you go black, you don't go back, like a white bitch quote. Hating to see a nigga make a million of these dope shit I wrote, and I quote, he will grow to be nothing but a hoodlum, end up in jail or someone will shoot him, high chased and deceased just to watch the police do him, I'm gone again, like 5 to 10, like nobody ever know him. This life will make the Death of me, balling out of control hoping these pigs don't get the best of me, I'm a Boss ain't no more testing me, ball till you fall, then ball again, I'm a Boss player I was Born to win, rolling up another bomb blunt just because it's on again, I'm human player potna I was born to sin.

Cocaine residue on my digital, chopping down coke next to a chop, loving that money when it rolls in no stop, a true to life hustla I can't stop, loving the stop of that pistol pop, my grind is like getting a Dope friend to stop, hard like a tip to top, my game on strong like when you can't that pit to stop, your neighborhood Dope Man pit stop, place that on your triple beam and slang it only pull that K out to aim it, safety off when I cock back to flame it, I'm a soul you can't tame, I'm real and these lame, that's why real niggas like me cock back to aim, you flame, it's nothing to me, a true Boss is what I claim to be, ain't no flinching when they cock back and aim at me, the realest nigga talking until the end of me, a Boss like I pretend to be, if you really need a hitta, send for me, it ain't nothing but a trip to me, just another million dollar hustla to grip for me, one through the dome and it's for me, just another million dollar pack sent to me, all the real Killas put your guns up, and blast on these bustas just to get your funds up, I guess the fun's up. I'm a boss daring these niggas to run up, hustling on the Block from sun down to sun up, hustling on the Block from sun down to sun up, a true Dope slanging gun toata putting sugar in your motor, your can't fuck with me, I'm your OG's OG, stick to your guns homeboy, that's what the Dope Game told me, forever feeling like these niggas owe me, I'm a hustla count me in, I'm putting heads down in the dirt if I find the penn, just ask the Ball or next to you homie, it feels so good to win, you ball till you fall, then you Ball again, I shine to win, just dust yourself off then try again I win even when I don't try to win, I'm not under contract but I can find a pen, tell the homie it's on again, these niggas paying 100 for 5 and 2 for 40 with no slack, thinking to myself this is how you get back, the world is a pussy and it hit that, the world is mine, a quarter mill with no time, all I need is a punch to shine, so beauty on the line, I'm sitting a trillion dollar grind, and it ain't not more nickel and dime, I don't know about you but I to shine, swimming in money like I lost my mind, homie this world is mine.

POEM

A day late and dollar short, watching my dreams fly right out the window, money on my mine like rain, sleet hail and snow, looking down at my self-wondering where did the time go, where did my mind go, running in circles day after day, watching my life float away, where were you when the rain came, just look at what I became, bothered, cared, and slaved, ain't no more love for me, holding lose to promises of the past, but we all know that promises won't last, stuck in the future, caught up by the past watching the hours past, tell me how long will this pain last, I bring up the past, falling in love with the pain, drowning in the rain of my own sorrows, stuck in the wind, knowing I can win again and again but when will my pain end, how could you forget me, this man of flesh, without you there's nothing left, and I'm running out of breath, will you remember me, when I'm gone. Here until thy Father calls me Home GOODBYE Love, I'M GONE, (but never forgotten), a day late and a dollar.

KUSH

I know niggas that hate their momma, but love Kushy I want to give the bomb game a push, presidents of the Cannabis club like George Bush, niggas I push Kush just ask my momma, come to Cali baby boy and I'll Bomb ya, the cure for what L's you, you ain't a true bomb, smoker if I don't smell ya, ain't telling what them other niggas will sell ya, I'm a true OG homie. I don't know what else to tell you, real G's don't fuck with the seeds, we put the system's together and push trees, sitting back watching babies grow, I'm a genius I told you so. I use to be illegal like pre probation now, prescribing medicine is the mission, make a mill off medicine a cooking THC in the Kitchen wise up little nigga Listen sewing up the world's with bombbay is the mission, giving the Kush a push, dropping bombs on the world like George Bush, Baby boy I'm in love with the Kush.

In the beginning, a spark of light to life, something more than understanding, my mind more extraordinary, living a life less ordinary, here before what you call earth, born from a different birth, somewhere between the lines of heaven, and earth, my mind, like the land, and sea, here before this land of earth, hearing screams of what life is afterbirth, my thoughts of man of earth, listening to the beginnings of man and earth, combining with ripening hands the sand of earth, delicate like a seamstress with hand to shirt, ahead in mind and birth devouring time, and space in your time, and year, in love with life. Living a life before fear forever present in your time, and year. Tossing to engagements, feeling a different part completes life, the beginning in art, sculpting life and the feelings of heart, bless those blessed with the man marked, visions of those blessed with more meaning in heart, through life, and pen, correcting error after error after life's end again and again. Bless those who give the meaning to meaning and the ability of understanding, understanding man's love of hate, understanding the cycles and patterns of life, watching life consume life to begin life again, what a deadly game men you play, watching this life of sin, and a man's love for a life more tempting, something more than your understanding, something more than the winds of mind and knowing, completely complete in mind, and knowing, amused by the understanding of the winds blowing, try to understand the mind of knowing, something greater than life, and understanding greater than what the eyes are showing, visions of something greater than what the eyes are showing, visions of something greater than pleasure and pain, and understanding greater than mankind, greater than the pleasure of mind in the beginning, vision older than space, and time, an understanding older than mankind, understand the meanings of life, I understand there's more than fear to life. Bless those who search for the spark that brought forth the light, as light still brings fourth the spark to life.

I bring forth the power to bring white to life the power to turn cream to white, whip up, stack up and turn this cream to white, me, my piece, half a million and his key of white, this is the type of shit that can bring your dreams to life, I can change the world with a Key of white, whisper in a bitch car drum, and bring her dreams to life, what you know, I got bitches playing with they pussy throwing their panties out the window, Baby I am bringing your dreams to life, the realest nigga talking, haters talk shit, but that money is still walking, rise like a Gee and let my strap to the talking. I can change the world with a Key of white, I'm an OG today and tonight, balling like the only nigga to dip that cream to life, my nigga hustling is the only way to bring your dreams to life, my triple beam is a Dope friend to life. I can change the world with a G white, now what you think I'd stack off a key of white, I'm zone tight bringing dope friends to life. I'm done spitting this cream to life, and whipping this cream to white. That's why I got the hotel room with kitchen, money coming cause I got my palms itching, these niggas could make mill is listening, never forget profit is the mission, that's why niggas break you down, cut it up and cook it in the kitchen, and I can white this, and can white that, and it started with a dough sac. I'm the realest nigga alive I already told you that, I can change the world with a key of white, if you can't play boy, I can cut your key tonight, whipping this cream to white. I'm a hustla baby, is there anything you like, I am ready hope you keep your pussy tight, getting head off the profit off a Key, it's all just another day into the life, like white to me, niggas 24-7 hustla day, and night for me, here until they take this life from me hoping they don't take this white from me. I'm a grown Man, fuck these niggas not liking me, I'd rather count the profit off a key, the realest nigga talking, these niggas ain't fucking with me, I told you baby, I can bring your dreams to life, I'm just a Boss this cream to white.

I push rhymes and slang dope, rubber banding stacks, inhaling bomb down my throat, with every live that wrote, showing these niggas hard to get a bird to float, ball till I fall and then its back to slanging dope, watching the cream sink to the bottom, as the water stays afloat, grew up around niggas that only hustla, and slang dope, spitting game, and nines with a twist, letting these suckas know they can't fuck with this, I wonder if you can see the lime through mists. I'm so pimptastic with a gangsta twist like a lion in the mist. I push rhymes and slang dope to cope, drinking Bombay watching murder she wrote, laid back thinking of this life of dope. I feel like I lost all of my friends and family, and it's hard to cope, drowning my sorrows by slanging dope, and this extra clip. I tote, this isn't just another rap song to quote, I spit my life to the best, like the pistol I tote, my fish scale ain't a joke. I just take a sniff and taste the cream slide down your throat, I'm Dope, this world with a Key, I'm Hot like the whole world against me. Cause I BIG, strapped up for life, nigga it's them against me, shocking niggas back to life, hating hit by that flash of light, fucking with niggas, gambling they 25 to life, all over respect changing that dope price, niggas that push rhymes and slang dope to cope, fuck a nine to five momma, I'd rather slang dope, I push rhymes life weight, shoot first don't hesitate, remembering how my nigga taught me how to turn soft to cake, nigga I can mill out of shake, fucking with nigga that don't give, and take nigga you skimp the cake, just a word to the wise. You are not supposed to shake a bake and double up the money you make.

I've seen the hate turn to love

Love turn to hate

And water turn to wine,

Slanging game because if you give them

What they really want

They'll hate you

Remember you always commit

Up until they know you down

Remember I haven't seen a Christmas

In about ten years, riding, listening to pac

Lunics call me the Don

And not matter what you say

I make Black people look

Good and I won't stop

I try to wish good luck

To the next man,

But they never do they same for me

Never believing in bullshit because

It don't play off.

Blasting off as I continue to grind

And never show love to those who continue to have me

I was listening to the wind and I hope they aren't hating

On my play pot and like they do me

Living life to the fullest, until deat I hope when I die I come back again.

Ducking and dodging these misdemeanors

Capture and the feds.

Inhaling marijuana stronger than cocaine

I love my momma, and I cant talkback yesterday

Sometimes it feels like I missed my whole life time

Playing Russian roulette without the win at the end

Don't get you and your loud smoked like they murdered my familu

And wouldn't let me bring them back to what can I say.

I love myself Geeking.

In hacking the smoke from a cigar a rolled myself retarded

Got four or five siblings but me and my momma,

All I ever had

March 2019

I can still remember when I sold my first E-Book

and immortalized my name in light

Beating up modern day slavery

With the best of my ability

And everybody wants to fuck my bitch

I picked this collection of songs and poems to inspire the world with my expression and view of life from my point of view. I started writing these pieces of art many years ago when I was surrounded by hater in a great time of need. I had to take a journey inside myself and create my own happiness and these songs, poems, and information poured out through a pen, helping me in a great time of need. I wanted to share with you the reader this collection of ideas, hoping to entertain and tickle the imagination of the world. The creation of this collection was a great step in the right direction in a great time of need. I am pleased with the outcome of this collection and hope to bring greater understanding peace, love, happiness and entertainment to you the reader in this great journey called life.

Printed in the United States
By Bookmasters